Pokémon™

BLACK AND WHITE

VOL. 11

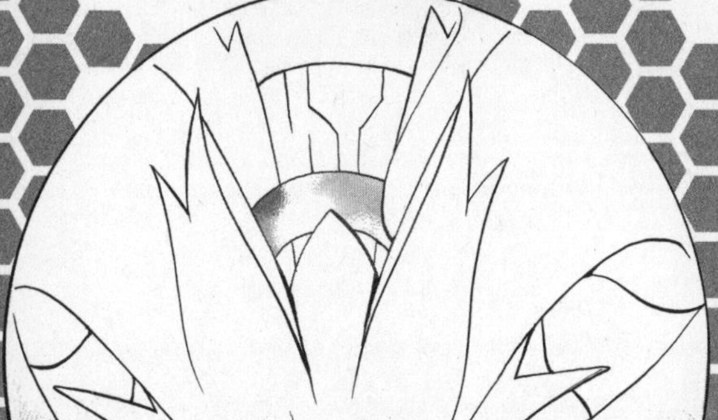

Story by HIDENORI KUSAKA
Art by SATOSHI YAMAMOTO

POKÉMON™
BLACK AND WHITE

Pokémon Black and White
Volume 11
VIZ Kids Edition

Story by HIDENORI KUSAKA
Art by SATOSHI YAMAMOTO

English Adaptation / Bryant Turnage
Translation / Tetsuichiro Miyaki
Touch-up & Lettering / Susan Daigle-Leach
Cover Art Assist / Kaillash Black, Walden Wong
Design / Fawn Lau
Editor / Annette Roman

Printed in the U.S.A.

Published by VIZ Media, LLC
P.O. Box 77010
San Francisco, CA 94107

10 9 8 7 6 5 4 3 2 1
First printing, August 2013

POKÉMON™

BLACK AND WHITE

VOL. 11

Adventure 35

THE BATTLE WITHIN 05

Adventure 36

MUSEUM SHOWDOWN 31

Adventure 37

FINDING TRUTH 57

THE STORY THUS FAR!

Pokémon Trainer Black is exploring the mysterious Unova region with his brand-new Pokédex. Pokémon Trainer White runs a thriving talent agency for performing Pokémon. While traveling together, their paths cross with Team Plasma, a nefarious group that advocates releasing your Pokémon into the wild! Now Black and White are off on their own separate journeys of discovery...

BLACK'S dream is to win the Pokémon League!

WHITE'S dream is to make her Tepig Gigi a star!

Black's Munna, MUSHA, helps him think clearly by temporarily "eating" his dream.

White's Tepig, GIGI, and Black's Pignite, NITE, get along like peanut butter and jelly! But now Gigi has left White for another Trainer...

Adventure 35
The Battle Within

THE NACRENE MUSEUM...
bamft
bamft
bamft
EXCUSE ME...
tmp

THE ENTRANCE IS ON THE FIRST FLOOR.
AND, UNFORTU-NATELY, THE MUSEUM IS CLOSED FOR THE DAY.
I'M LENORA, THE MUSEUM'S DIRECTOR.
AND I'M HAWES, HER HUSBAND AND ASSISTANT DIRECTOR.
HRMM...
WE KNOW WHO YOU ARE.
A MEMBER OF OUR ORGANIZATION WAS LUCKY ENOUGH TO HAVE SPOTTED A CERTAIN DRAGON-TYPE POKÉMON FOSSIL ON DISPLAY HERE—AN INCREDIBLE ARTIFACT...
OH, REAL-LY...?
PITY THAT IT WAS JUST AN ORDINARY DRAGON-TYPE POKÉMON FOSSIL.
WE'VE COME FOR THE REAL THING FOR...
...OUR KING! WE SEEK TO PROCURE THE DRAGON-TYPE POKÉMON INVOLVED IN THE CREATION OF UNOVA.

THE IDEALS OF UNOVA...
...THE *BLACK LIGHTNING BOLT*!!
thunk
WATCH OUT, HAWES!!
YOU'RE FROM TEAM PLASMA, AREN'T YOU?!
HA HA HA...
EX-ACTLY.
NOW, HAND OVER...

...THE DARK STONE...
HAND OVER...
...ZEK-ROM !!
GOOD! THIS IS GOING JUST AS WE PLANNED!!
NOW...
WE JUST NEED TO WAIT FOR...
...CLAY AND THE OTH-ERS!!
RRRGH! ANGRY... ANGRY... ANGRY...
CLAY... WE CAN TELL YOU'RE ANGRY. YOU DON'T HAVE TO KEEP SAYING IT.
TIMING IS EVERYTHING WITH THIS PLAN, YOU KNOW!!
WE'RE READY TO GO. WE ***HAVE*** TO GO...!
WHAT IS SKYLA ***DOING?!***

HER GYM BATTLE WITH BLACK IS TAKING LONGER THAN I EXPECTED.
WHAT ARE WE GONNA DO, BRYCEN?! GO TO THE GYM AND DRAG THEM OUT?!
NO. WAIT.
...
...
IF OUR PLAN FAILS, IT WAS MEANT TO FAIL FROM THE START.
AAAARGH!! YOU'RE ALL USELESS!!
Krash

HE DE-FEATED MY SWOO-BAT...
HA HA...
HOW'S THAT?!
catch
THANK YOU, SWOOBAT.
NEXT... SWANNA. GO!
flap flap
FOOM FOOM FOOM FOOM
DO IT, NITE!!
I'LL ATTACK OUR OPPONENT WITH EMBER... AND DELIVER THE FINISHING BLOW WITH HEAT CRASH!
I'LL USE THE SAME TACTIC!

FSZZZ
WATER SPORT!!
FSZZZ
FSZZZ
FSZZZ
BUBBLE-BEAM!!
I FORGOT THAT SWANNA IS A FLYING-TYPE AND WATER-TYPE POKÉMON!!
AAAH, NUTS!!
POP
POP
POP
POP
POP

I WAS TOLD YOU WERE A TRAINER WHO DID HIS HOMEWORK...
BUT YOUR BATTLE TECH-NIQUE IS AWFULLY SLOPPY.
GRRR...
BOM
COSTA !!
ANCIENT POWER!!
I HAVE TO PROVE MY SKILLS IN THIS BATTLE!!
AND THIS IS THE BEST MOVE I HAVE FOR THIS SITUA-TION!!
smash
krack
ka
thud

catch
THANK YOU, SWANNA.
GOOD!
slap
fwump
GO, UNFEZANT !!
flap flap
whoooooshh

S
WHAT ?!
CATCH
LAP
WHAT JUST HAP-PENED?
DID YOU... LOSE ?
IT'S NOT OVER YET!
WHAT ARE YOU DOING?
LEMME CHECK... THE OPPONENT WAS A FEMALE UNFEZANT. THE FLYING SKILLS OF THE FEMALE ARE SUPERIOR TO THE MALE AND...
OR ARE YOU GIVING UP?
READY TO GO HOME TO NUVEMA TOWN?!
NO WAY!!
TULA!
BOOM

slash
wff wff
wff
wff wff
pffttf fffft
TULA!!
UM... LOOKS LIKE ANY KIND OF THREAD WILL DO THE TRICK...
STRING SHOT !!
shoop
shoop
shoop
FLYING-TYPE POKÉMON ARE WEAK AGAINST ELECTRI-CALLY CHARGED THREADS.
YOU DO HAVE THE ADVANTAGE, BUT...

AND COS-TA...
THE UNFEZANT IS MUCH FASTER THAN I THOUGHT, BUT STILL...
THE ATTACK KEEPS MISSING THE TAR-GET!!
AS A MATTER OF FACT, IT WOULDN'T HAVE LEFT A SCRATCH IF COSTA HAD DEFENDED ITSELF!
THAT WAS PROBABLY AIR SLASH... BUT THAT MOVE ISN'T POWERFUL ENOUGH TO INFLICT A LOT OF DAMAGE ON COSTA.
UH-HUH... THAT'S WHAT IT LOOKED LIKE TO ME.
DID YOU *LET* YOURSELF GET HIT BY THAT ATTACK... ON PURPOSE?! BECAUSE YOU'RE UNHAPPY ABOUT SOMETHING ?!
WAIT...!
!!
...THE UNCLEAR SOUND OF THE BELL.
THIS MIGHT BE THE REASON BEHIND...

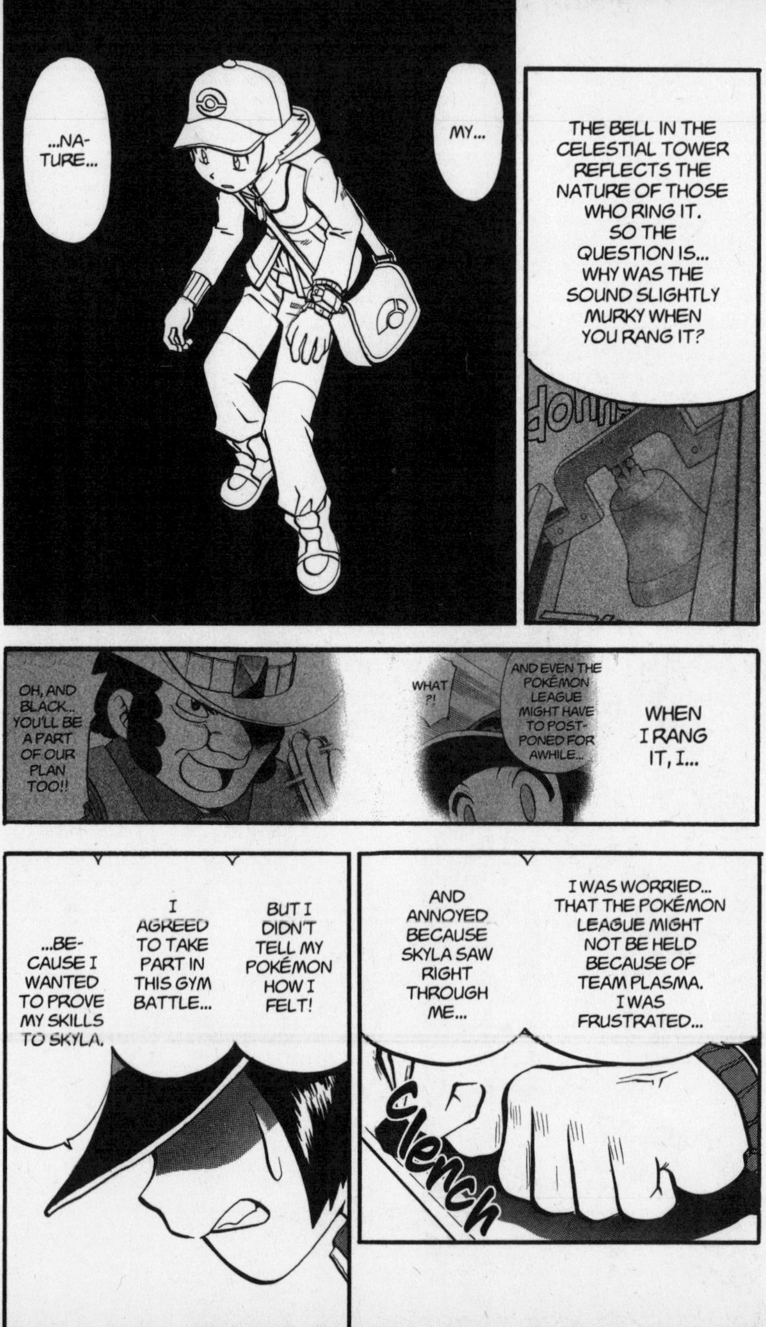

...NA-TURE...
MY...
THE BELL IN THE CELESTIAL TOWER REFLECTS THE NATURE OF THOSE WHO RING IT. SO THE QUESTION IS... WHY WAS THE SOUND SLIGHTLY MURKY WHEN YOU RANG IT?
OH, AND BLACK... YOU'LL BE A PART OF OUR PLAN TOO!!
WHAT?!
AND EVEN THE POKÉMON LEAGUE MIGHT HAVE TO POST-PONED FOR AWHILE...
WHEN I RANG IT, I...
...BE-CAUSE I WANTED TO PROVE MY SKILLS TO SKYLA.
I AGREED TO TAKE PART IN THIS GYM BATTLE...
BUT I DIDN'T TELL MY POKÉMON HOW I FELT!
AND ANNOYED BECAUSE SKYLA SAW RIGHT THROUGH ME...
I WAS WORRIED... THAT THE POKÉMON LEAGUE MIGHT NOT BE HELD BECAUSE OF TEAM PLASMA. I WAS FRUSTRATED...
Clench

TULA!!
WE'LL NEED TO GIVE IT OUR ALL...
...TO DEFEAT THEM!!
NITE, MUSHA, COSTA— LISTEN UP!!
I WANT TO ENTER THE POKÉMON LEAGUE WITH YOU GUYS! AND ***THAT'S*** WHY I WANT TO BE A PART OF THIS PLAN TO DEFEAT TEAM PLASMA!!
JUMP
kzzzttttzzz

SKYLA!!
tmp tmp tmp
grin
ffrummbl
rmmmmm
WE'RE TAKING OFF NOW. PLEASE TAKE YOUR SEATS AND FASTEN YOUR SEAT-BELTS SECURE-LY...
HEY! WHERE'S BLACK...?! HOW DID THE GYM BATTLE TURN OUT?!

HUH ...?
rmmmbl
WHA–?
WHY...
...DID SHE LEAVE WITHOUT ME?
I WON...
...MY GYM BATTLE!!
tink
UM...
WHAT'S ...
...GO-ING...
tink
tnk
...ON ?!

WHAT'S HAPPEN-ING?!
shunk
OW.
shunk
OOF.
shunk
ACK.
shunk
OUCH ...

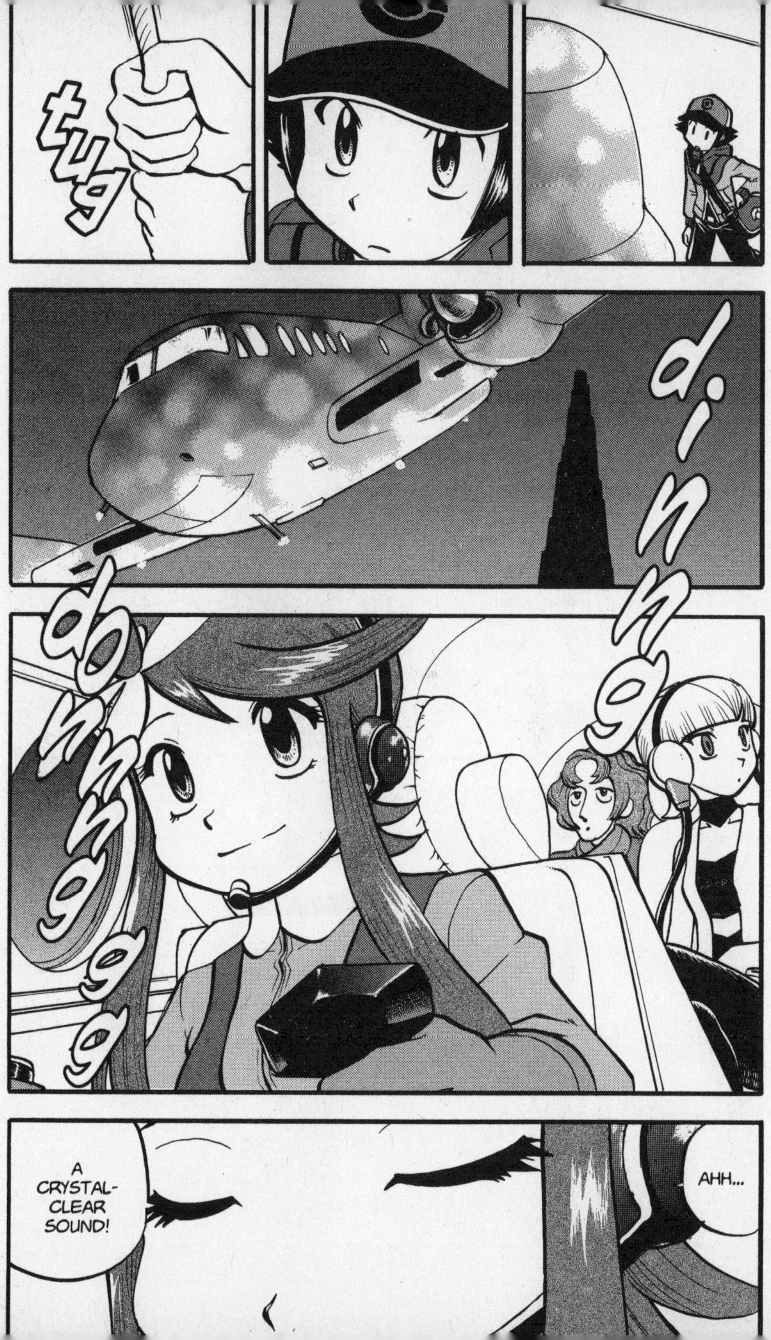
tug
dinng
donnngg
A CRYSTAL-CLEAR SOUND!
AHH...

BOM
roaaarr
turn
plink
AND YOU MANAGED TO RING THE BELL WITH A CLEAR SOUND— ONE THAT WILL SOOTHE THE SOULS OF THE POKÉMON RESTING HERE.
rmmbbl
OF COURSE! YOU WON, BLACK.
FOR ME?!
THE JET BADGE!!

I WOULD LOVE FOR YOU TO AID US ON THIS MISSION...
...TO PROTECT THE DARK STONE!
LET'S GO!!
jump
TO NA-CRENE!!
kr-a-sh

IT'S OVER. GIVE IT UP.
DO YOU REALLY BELIEVE YOU TWO CAN FEND US ALL OFF BY YOUR-SELVES?
WE WERE JUST WAITING FOR YOU TO LOWER YOUR SECURITY LEVEL.
WHAT THE...?!
WHAT TOOK YOU SO LONG?!
IT'S NOT OVER YET!!

fsssh
tmp
tmp
tmp

PREMIER INSECT ARTIST...
...BURGH!
THE SHINING BEAUTY...
...ELESA.
THE UNDERGROUND BOSS...
...CLAY!
THE HIGH-FLYING GIRL...
...SKYLA!
...
AND...
...AN ARCHEOLOGIST WITH BACKBONE.
LENORA!

LOWERING THE SECURITY LEVEL... YOU DID THAT ON PURPOSE?!
YOU LURED US DOWN HERE...
...WHILE SECRETLY GATHERING YOUR FORCES NEARBY!!
THAT'S RIGHT!!
WE WILL NEVER LET...
...TEAM PLASMA...
...HAVE THE DARK STONE!!
THE BATTLE IS STARTING...!!

Adventure 36
Museum Showdown

charge
SKYLA !!
WHAM
PATRAT-RETALIATE!!
DASH

OKAY!
RAZOR WIND!!
slash

rmbl rmbl rmbl rmbl
THEIR COMBINATION ATTACKS ARE AMAZING!!
LENORA'S BATTLE SKILLS ARE EVEN MORE IMPRESSIVE THAN THE LAST TIME!!
THANKS FOR FLYING ME HERE, SWANNA!!
YOUR JOB IS INSIDE THE MUSEUM!
LEAVE THIS TO US. WE'LL TAKE CARE OF TEAM PLASMA.
LONG TIME NO SEE, BLACK! NOT SINCE OUR GYM BATTLE...
fwip fwip
ON MY WAY!!
I NEED HELP OVER HERE! TEAM PLASMA HAS BROKEN THROUGH THE BACK DOOR!

IT'S NOT OVER HERE!!
HAS ANYONE FOUND IT?!
NO, NOT YET!!
EVERY-ONE SEARCH IN THERE!
THE LIBRARY AREA IN THE BACK LOOKS SUSPI-CIOUS!
HMPH! THOSE GYM LEADERS ARE SO SNEAKY!!
WHERE DID THEY HIDE IT?!
ka-smash
STOP! GET OUT OF HERE!

YOU'LL NEVER GET THE DARK STONE... OR ZEKROM!!
EMBER!!
BRINE!!
ELECTROWEB!!
IF YOUR EVIL PLAN TO RELEASE A LEGENDARY DRAGON-TYPE POKÉMON STANDS IN THE WAY OF MY DREAM OF WINNING THE POKÉMON LEAGUE...
...THEN I'LL DO EVERYTHING IN MY POWER...
...TO CRUSH YOU!!

thunk
thunk
UNBE-LIEV-ABLE...
YOU GYM LEADERS...
...DECEIVED US!
LET'S SEE... SIX OF THEM.
THREE OF US.
THAT MEANS WE EACH TAKE ON TWO!
YOU FIGHT CLAY AND ELESA.
I'LL DEAL WITH LENORA AND SKYLA.
AND YOU GET...
...BURGH AND BRYCEN... ALL RIGHT?
ALL SET ...?
dash
GO!!

I'LL DRILL HOLES INTO YOU BEFORE YOU EVEN GET THE CHANCE TO ATTACK!!
thud
LILLIGANT! QUIVER DANCE!!
spinzzz
grab
boing
EMOLGA—ACRO-BATICS!!
slash
MEGA DRAIN!!
fwazoop

THANKS, ELESA!
EVEN THOUGH WE OUT-NUMBER THEM, I CAN'T AFFORD TO LET MY GUARD DOWN!
DEFEAT...
...IS THE FATE OF THOSE...
...PUFFED-UP WITH PRIDE.
A MAR-TIAL ARTS STANCE ...
COME TO THINK OF IT... ISN'T THERE A FORMER ACTION MOVIE STAR WHO BECAME A GYM LEADER...? WHO WAS FORCED TO RETIRE FROM SHOW BUSINESS AFTER GETTING INJURED...? WHAT A SAD HAS-BEEN!
...

YAA!!
krikk krikk krikkr
fwoosh
OOH!!
THE ICE AND FIRE ATTACKS ARE CLASHING!! BUT...
...BRYCEN IS CLEARLY AT A DISADVANTAGE!
YOUR ICE HAS TURNED TO HARMLESS CRYSTALS BEFORE IT COULD EVEN REACH ME!!
PATHETIC...
WHAT?!
YOU USE VERBAL ATTACKS IN A VAIN ATTEMPT TO SHAKE-UP YOUR OPPONENT...
A COWARDLY STRATEGY.

THE LIKES OF YOU...
...CAN NEVER RATTLE ME.
Yank
WHAT?!

A CHAIN—OF ICE!
AMA-ZING !!
SQUEEZE
WHEN DID YOU CREATE THIS?!
CRYOGONAL ORIGINATE FROM ARCTIC CLOUDS—AND THEY CAPTURE THEIR PREY WITH CHAINS OF ICE.
BRYCEN USED LARVESTA'S FIRE TO SHATTER THE ICE...
...CAUSING THE ICE CRYSTALS TO FLY THROUGH THE AIR AND CREATE THAT CHAIN!
GRRR !!
I NEED YOUR HELP!!

AQUA TAIL !!
slap slap slap
HYPER BEAM !!
booshbooshbooshboosh
YOUR POKÉ-MON JUST MELT-ED AWAY !!
HEH HEH HEH !!
wom
wom
wom
IT DISAP-PEARED—YES. HOW-EVER...

CRYOGONAL HAS TURNED INTO WATER VAPOR...
AND NOW ...!!
ffff
ffff
...
COMPLE-TION!
jingle

Wrap
WHAT AN ARTISTIC AND FANTASTIC BATTLE!!
BRYCEN CER-TAINLY IS POWER-FUL!
THIS IS THE FIRST TIME I'VE SEEN HIM IN BATTLE!
WON-DER-FUL!!
YEAH! AND HE'S THE ONLY ONE WHO HASN'T BEEN INJURED!
GURGH ...!!
GRR!
WE MUST NOT...
WE MUST NOT FAIL. WE MUST PROCURE THE DARK STONE FOR OUR KING!

"KING," HUH ...?
IN FACT, DIDN'T YOU USE THE SAME WORDS WHEN YOU ARRIVED...?
BABBLING SOMETHING ABOUT "FOR OUR KING... THE DRAGON-TYPE POKÉMON!"...
THIS KING MUST BE THE BOSS OF TEAM PLASMA!!
WELL THEN... YOU'RE GONNA GUIDE US TO...
...YOUR SO-CALLED "KING"! AND TO YOUR HEAD-QUARTERS!!
THAT WON'T HAPPEN.
WE'VE STAKED EVERYTHING ON THIS MISSION...
RMBL RMBL RMBL RMBL RMBL RM
?!

THAT'S HALF OF THEM DOWN!
BUT THERE ARE STILL MORE IN THE LIBRARY IN BACK!
rmmbl rmm bl
THE MUSEUM IS SHAKING!
rm bbl
I'VE FELT THIS... ...BE-FORE...
rmbl
CLAY! WHAT'S HAPPEN-ING?!!
STAY INSIDE!! YOU SHOULDN'T HAVE COME OUT HERE!!
fwip

rm
bl
mmm

AHHHHHHH!
TORNADUS!
THUNDURUS!
EVEN LANDORUS!
THE LEGENDARY POKÉMON MY GRAND-MOTHER TOLD ME ABOUT...
I CAN'T BELIEVE TEAM PLASMA CAP-TURED...
...ALL THREE OF THEM!!
...!!
CLAY!!
I TOLD YOU TO STAY PUT!!
HAVE YOU FORGOTTEN WHAT LENORA ASKED OF YOU?!

BUT, BUT—
DON'T GET TOO FULL OF YOURSELF, BLACK!!
YOU MIGHT THINK BEATING SIX OF US MAKES YOU OUR EQUAL...
...BUT YOU'RE STILL AN ORDINARY TRAINER—NOT A GYM LEADER!!
drip
JUST DO AS YOU WERE TOLD AND PROTECT THE MUSEUM!!
YOU CAN'T HELP US HERE!!!
AH...
AH...
AAH...!!
AAAAH!!!
dash
zip

kick
smash
grab
shattr
squeeze
NITE ...!!
ting ting ting
krak

IT AP-PEARS THE TIDE HAS TURNED.
THERE'S NOTHING YOU CAN DO NOW.
EXCEPT MAKE YOUR EXIT...
WOM
NO...
WOM
NO !!!
WOM

CHUNK
TA

THE DRAGONSPIRAL TOWER...
THIS TOWER WAS BUILT LONG BEFORE UNOVA CAME TO BE...
AND ON THE VERY TOP FLOOR...
...A BATTLE WAS FOUGHT BETWEEN...
...IDEALS AND TRUTH.

Adventure 37
Finding Truth

LET THE GYM LEADERS GO!!
LANDO-RUS!
HA!
AND WHO'S GOING TO MAKE US?! A MERE BOY LIKE YOU...?

SMASH
FLICK
WE'VE CAPTURED THE GYM LEADERS.
THEY SET A TRAP FOR US...
...BUT IN THE END, THEY WERE NO MATCH FOR US.
EXCUSE US!

WE'VE SEARCHED EVERY CORNER OF THE MUSEUM ...!
BUT THE DARK STONE IS NOWHERE TO BE FOUND!!
NO-WHERE TO BE...
...FOUND?
YOU'RE THE ASSISTANT DIRECTOR OF THIS MUSEUM, AREN'T YOU?
chomp
chomp
WERE YOU LYING ALL ALONG ABOUT THE DARK STONE BEING IN YOUR POSSESSION?
NO... THAT CAN'T BE RIGHT.
THERE'S A SECRET ROOM AROUND HERE SOMEWHERE, ISN'T THERE?
ISN'T THERE ?!
Eeeek!
SO, YOU FIGURED IT OUT...
YOU'RE RIGHT.
THERE'S A BASEMENT ROOM WHERE I STORE ESPECIALLY VALUABLE BONES AND FOSSILS.
BUT THE ONLY KEY TO THE ROOM WAS DESTROYED BY THE ATTACK OF THUNDURUS, TORNADUS AND LANDORUS!

THAT BASEMENT IS BUILT LIKE A BUNKER. YOU'LL NEVER BE ABLE TO CRACK IT OPEN.
SEE THE ENTRANCE THERE? GO AHEAD AND TRY THIS KEY IN THE LOCK IF YOU DON'T BELIEVE ME.
OH, AND BY THE WAY...
tink tink tink
WHAT ?!
LANDORUS! THUNDURUS!! TORNADUS!!!
KAFOOM

NO NEED TO PANIC.
WHY, YOU ...!
IRONICALLY, IT SEEMS THAT USING SUCH POWERFUL POKÉMON HAS WORKED AGAINST YOU...
NOW YOU'LL NEVER BE ABLE TO GET YOUR HANDS ON THE DARK STONE!
WHAT DID I TELL YOU?
AND IF WE TAKE THE GYM LEADERS BACK WITH US, THERE'LL BE NO ONE LEFT TO INTERFERE WITH OUR PLANS!
THERE MUST BE A WAY.
DON'T BOTHER. HE'S HELPLESS ON HIS OWN.
WHAT SHOULD WE DO? GET RID OF HIM?
OH. I FORGOT ABOUT HIM.
march
march
RE-TREAT !!
WA... I... T...
NO...

CLAY!!
LENORA!!
BURGH! ELESA!
SKY-LA! BRY-CEN!

WOOOSH
WE LOST!
THEY TOTALLY TROUNCED US...
AND KIDNAPPED ALL THE GYM LEADERS TO BOOT!
WHAT DO I DO NOW...?!
THAT WINK LENORA GAVE ME... WHAT DID IT MEAN?

IT WAS LIKE...
...SHE WAS TELLING ME, "YOU TAKE CARE OF THE REST"...
THAT'S WHAT IT LOOKED LIKE, ANYWAY...
OH!
I'VE GOT IT!!
...
ARE YOU ALL RIGHT?

BRYCEN! HOW DID YOU ESCAPE?!
I SLIPPED OUT WHILE LENORA AND THE SHADOW TRIAD WERE TALKING...
THEY WEREN'T PAYING ATTENTION. THEY GOT OVER-CONFIDENT BECAUSE THEY WON THE BATTLE.
OH! BOY AM I GLAD TO SEE YOU!
THANKS... WHAT WERE YOU SAYING JUST NOW...?
OH YEAH! LENORA SAID...
...NO ONE COULD ENTER THE BASEMENT BECAUSE THE KEY WAS DESTROYED.
BUT I THINK THERE'S ANOTHER WAY DOWN THERE!!
WHAT MAKES YOU SAY THAT?
HEH...
brsh brsh
BECAUSE I GOT INTO THAT BASEMENT...
...ANOTHER WAY ONCE BEFORE!

THE STORAGE ROOM IN THE BASEMENT IS ALSO THE BATTLE ARENA FOR LENORA'S GYM BATTLES.
IT TOOK YOU JUST THREE MINUTES AND THIRTY SECONDS TO REACH MY OFFICE.
THAT'S WHERE I HAD MY GYM BATTLE WITH LENORA!
I GUESS LENORA USED HER PERSONAL ENTRANCE— THE ONE WITH THE BROKEN KEY NOW— TO GET DOWN THERE HERSELF.
BUT CHALLENGERS HAVE TO SOLVE A PUZZLE WHILE WALKING THROUGH A MAZE OF BOOKSHELVES TO FIND THE HIDDEN ENTRANCE.
HMM... I HAD NO IDEA NACRENE GYM HAD A GIMMICK LIKE THAT...
I SHOULD BE ABLE TO GET INTO THE BASEMENT BY FOLLOWING THE SAME ROUTE I USED LAST TIME!!
BUT LENORA DID SAY...
...IT WAS STRONG AS A BUNKER.
MAYBE IT'S SAFER TO JUST LEAVE IT THERE.
NO!
BEFORE THEY LEFT, TEAM PLASMA SAID, "THERE MUST BE A WAY."

WE HAVE NO WAY OF KNOWING HOW SOON THEY'LL RETURN WITH ENOUGH POWER TO BREAK THROUGH THE WALLS OF THAT BUNKER!
I SAY WE MOVE THE DARK STONE TO A NEW HIDING PLACE AS SOON AS WE CAN!
RIGHT!
DO YOU REMEMBER HOW TO SOLVE THE MAZE?
I'LL GIVE IT A TRY. MUSHA!
glomp
I HAVE TO REMEMBER! HAVE TO REMEMBER...
THAT'S IT...!
My First Pokémon
FIRST, IT WAS THE BOOK-SHELF IN THE CENTER ROW... AND THEN...
TWO FROM THE BACK ...
fwip
ONE TO THE LEFT...
TWO TO THE FRONT ...

SO...
PUSH
AND I'M THE ONLY ONE WHO KNOWS— BECAUSE I'M AN ORDINARY POKÉMON TRAINER!
I'VE HAD A GYM BATTLE AT THE NACRENE GYM, SO I KNOW HOW TO ENTER THE SECRET BASEMENT.
THIS WAS WHY THE GYM LEADERS ASKED ME TO PARTICIPATE IN THEIR PLAN!
AND WHY THEY TOLD ME TO STAY INSIDE THE MUSEUM!
rmbl
rmbl
NOW THAT THE GYM LEADERS HAVE BEEN DEFEATED, IT'S MY JOB TO PROTECT THE DARK STONE!
bl
rmbl
I'VE GOT TO ESCAPE WITH THE DARK STONE!! THAT'S WHAT LENORA WAS TRYING TO TELL ME!!
!!
fwip
fwip
YES... I SEE...

FOUND IT!! THAT'S...
...THE DARK STONE!!
...THE DARK STONE.
THAT IS IN-DEED...
RIGHT.
RIGHT, BRYCEN...?!
HUH?
WHO'S THERE?!

KRAKAZZZ
twitch
twitch
drop
BRY-CEN...!
WHY...?
flump
BRY-CEN?
THERE'S...
...NO ONE HERE BY THAT NAME.
TEAM PLAS-MA...
donk
A DIS-GUISE...?
BEHOLD THE DARK STONE...

YES. I AM GHETSIS, ONE OF THE SEVEN SAGES...
...OF TEAM PLASMA.
GHETSIS!!

...THE DARK STONE !!
I... I LED YOU... STRAIGHT TO...
THANK YOU. WE WOULD NEVER HAVE BEEN ABLE TO ENTER THIS ROOM WITHOUT YOU.
AND IT'S NOT AS IF YOU CAN DO ANY-THING TO STOP US NOW.
DON'T STAND UP. YOU NEED TO GET SOME REST.
I AM SURE OUR KING WILL BE MOST GRATEFUL.
WE MUST BE OFF IMMEDI-ATELY.
I HAVE NO TIME TO WASTE.
FWUMP
...FAILED...
I...

MY KING...
I APOLOGIZE FOR THE LONG WAIT.
I PRESENT TO YOU... ***THE DARK STONE.***
I HAVE BEEN WAITING QUITE SOME TIME FOR YOU...
THE DRAGON-TYPE POKÉMON FROM THE FOUNDING OF UNOVA... THE DEEP BLACK POKÉMON OF IDEALS...

REVIVE FROM THE STONE YOU TRANSFORMED YOURSELF INTO...
RETURN TO YOUR TRUE FORM!
UNLEASH YOURSELF!
AND TOGETHER WITH ME, N...
...WE WILL CREATE A UTOPIAN HOME FOR LIBERATED POKÉMON...
...MY ZEKROM!!

IT IS I...
...GHET-SIS!
WHERE ARE YOU NOW?
WE'RE ON OUR WAY TO THE CASTLE.
WHAT OF THE GYM LEADERS?
WE HAVE CAPTURED SIX OF THEM—PLUS LENORA'S HUSBAND.
UH-OH...
WAIT!!
THIS ONE IS...
...JUST AN ICE SCULP-TURE!
WHAT...?
MY APOLOGIES, SIR! ONE OF THEM HAS ESCAPED!
BRYCEN... THE GYM LEADER OF ICCIRUS CITY!
HMM. HE'S RATHER CRAFTY, IT SEEMS.
BUT UN-FORTU-NATELY FOR HIM...
...IT IS...
...ALREADY TOO LATE.

SOMEONE DISGUISED AS *ME*...
...TRICKED BLACK!
AND STOLE ...
...THE DARK STONE!
BY NOW, IT COULD ALREADY BE TURNED BACK INTO ZEKROM!
SHUNK
blip

OPE-LUC-ID CITY ...
DRAY-DEN SPEAK-ING.
I SEE ...
WHAT ABOUT THE OTHER STONE?
rmbl
blip
THE LIGHT STONE...
...IS HERE.
LUCKILY THEY HAD NO INKLING THAT WE KEPT THE LIGHT STONE AT THE SAME LOCATION.
IF THEY'VE AWAKENED ZEKROM FROM THE DARK STONE... THE WHOLE WORLD IS IN PERIL.
THIS WASN'T A PART OF OUR PLAN, BUT... IF THAT'S THE CASE, WE'LL HAVE TO TRANSFORM THE LIGHT STONE INTO...

...THE LEGENDARY VAST WHITE POKÉMON THAT REPRESENTS TRUTH...
...RESHI-RAM!
roll
AFTER THAT...
AND THEN...
ting
roll
roll
tunk
tunk
tunk
BRYCEN...?

WHAT'S WRONG, BRYCEN?! ARE YOU LISTENING TO ME?
...
THAT'S FINE. I'M COUNTING ON YOU, DRAYDEN...
I HAVE NO IDEA WHAT'S GOING TO HAPPEN NOW...
BUT WHATEVER IT IS...
...LOOKS LIKE I HAVE NO CHOICE BUT TO TRAIN YOU.
IT'S GOING TO BE REALLY TOUGH...
I HOPE YOU CAN KEEP UP, KID!

More Adventures COMING SOON...

Team Plasma has kidnapped all but two of the Unova gym leaders! Before he can help rescue the others, Black must undergo grueling training. Will it be enough now that Team Plasma has awakened dangerous Legendary Pokémon Zekrom...?! Meanwhile, White's new battle skills are put to the test when Bianca needs help protecting an innocent Pokémon...

THEN, WILL BIANCA DISCOVER HER *OWN* DREAM...?

Plus, meet Cryogonal, Vullaby, Meloetta and...*Emboar*?!

VOL. 12 AVAILABLE OCTOBER 2013!

ARCEUS HAS BEEN BETRAYED—
NOW THE WORLD IS IN DANGER!
Long ago, the mighty Pokémon Arceus was betrayed by a human it trusted. Now Arceus is back for revenge! Dialga, Palkia and Giratina must join forces to help Ash, Dawn and their new friends Kevin and Sheena stop Arceus from destroying humankind. But it may already be too late!
Seen the movie? Read the manga!
vizkids
Pokémon
ARCEUS
AND THE
JEWEL OF LIFE
Story and Art by
Makoto Mizobuchi
Original Concept by Satoshi Tajiri
Supervised by Tsunekazu Ishihara
Script by Hideki Sonoda
Pokémon
ARCEUS
AND THE
JEWEL OF LIFE
MANGA PRICE: $7.99 usa $9.99 can
ISBN-13: 9781421538020 • IN STORES FEBUARY 2011
Check out the complete library of Pokémon books at VIZ.com
© 2011 Pokémon.
© 1997-2011 Nintendo, Creatures, GAME FREAK, TV Tokyo, ShoPro, JR Kikaku. © Pikachu Project 2009.
Pokémon properties are trademarks of Nintendo.
ARUSEUS CHOUKOKU NO JIKUU E © 2009 Makoto MIZOBUCHI/Shogakukan
vk
VIZ media
RATED A FOR ALL AGES
www.vizkids.com
www.viz.com
ratings.viz.com

What's Better Than Catching Pokémon?
Becoming one!
Pokémon®
Mystery Dungeon
GINJI'S RESCUE TEAM
Ginji is a normal boy until the day he turns into a Torchic and joins Mudkip's Rescue Team. Now he must help any and all Pokémon in need...but will Ginji be able to rescue his human self?
Pokémon
Mystery Dungeon
GINJI'S RESCUE TEAM
Inspired by the brand-new Nintendo games
RED RESCUE TEAM
BLUE RESCUE TEAM
Story and art by
Makoto Mizobuchi
Become part of the adventure—and mystery—with *Pokémon Mystery Dungeon: Ginji's Rescue Team.* Buy yours today!
www.pokemon.com
viz media
www.viz.com
vizkids
© 2006 Pokémon. © 1995-2006 Nintendo/Creatures Inc./GAME FREAK inc.
© 1993-2006 CHUNSOFT. TM & ® are trademarks of Nintendo.
© 2006 Makoto MIZOBUCHI/Shogakukan Inc.
Cover art subject to change.

Backwards Game
BAKÉGYAMON

THIS IS THE END OF THIS GRAPHIC NOVEL!

To properly enjoy this VIZ Media graphic novel, please turn it around and begin reading from right to left.

This book has been printed in the original Japanese format in order to preserve the orientation of the original artwork. Have fun with it!

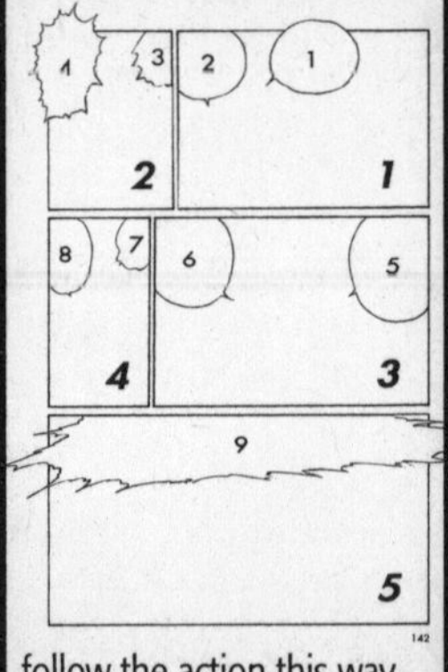

follow the action this way.